3 KIDS DREAMIN'

written by

LINDA ENGLAND

illustrations by

DENA SCHUTZER

MARGARET K. McELDERRY BOOKS

MARGARET K. McELDERRY BOOKS
25 YEARS • 1972–1997

Margaret K. McElderry Books
An imprint of Simon & Schuster Children's Publishing Division
1230 Avenue of the Americas
New York, New York 10020

Book design by Angela Carlino

The text of this book is set in Imperfect Bold

The illustrations are rendered in black crayon and ink

ISBN 978-14424-2944-4

Printed and bound in the United States of America

First Edition

10 9 8 7 6 5 4 3 2 1

Library of Congress Cataloging-in-Publication Data
England, Linda.
3 Kids Dreamin' / Linda England ; illustrated by Dena Schutzer. — 1st ed.
p. cm.
Summary: The story, told in rap, of three friends who find a place where their music is appreciated.
[1. Bands (Music)—Fiction. 2. Rap (Music)—Fiction.]
I. Schutzer, Dena, ill. II. Title.
PZ7.E713Sq 1997
[Fic]—dc20 95-45469
CIP AC

To Joe for freedom
Chris for listening
Betsy for sharing
Dad for my love of words and music
–L.E.

For Emma and Ben
–D.S.

Rockin'

Tumblin'

Slidin'

Shiftin'

Rollin'

We're a group called

Squeezed.

Ramone ticklin' the guitar

Willie talkin' the rap

Yock hammerin' the drums

Rhythm.

Willie says, "I'm talkin'

I'm rhymin'

I'm singin' sweet.

I'm tellin' the story of kids on the street.

I'm talkin' the words to the city's beat,

rappin'."

Ramone's movin' a thousand fingers,

pluckin' fireworks from steel strings.

Slidin' up and down the long neck of

the guitar.

High-pitched screams

Low moanin' sighs

Electric sounds.

Yock's bangin' those drumsticks

tappin' those drumsticks

rollin' those drumsticks

against the big drum's hide.

Sounds come growlin'

and hummin'

and thunderin'

from the drum's inside.

ON'T
WALK

Yock's mom yells, "Shut up,

Baby's goin' to sleep.

My basement isn't no music place."

Yock's sticks answer angry sounds

hammerin'

smackin'

bangin' against old basement

pipe sounds.

One yellow lightbulb hangin'

on a cord.

Swingin', swayin'

A slow rhythm of dull light

catchin'

Willie's face

Yock's face

and then Ramone's.

Feelin' the blue

down

blues.

Ramone's voice

soft

cool

"I know a man

A blind man

An old man,

Mr. Moses

"Bass" Smith.

He'll know

He'll know

A place for us

A place to be

rappin'

pickin'

boomin' beat.

We're

Squeezed."

New light of morning

Happy—their walkin' says so

Ramone

Yock and Willie

Tappin' feet

Rappin' words

Goin' to see the old man

goin' up Two Street

slappin' awnings

all the way.

Sittin' in an old chair

Mr. Moses "Bass" Smith

listenin'

Radio moanin' blues.

Mr. Moses smilin'

when the bass man plays

rememberin'

smilin' the dreams

of an old bass man.

Three fists

knockin'.

Ramone askin',

"Please, Mr. Smith

Came to ask

a place to play

to sing

to be."

Willie movin'

leg to leg

Yock singin' quiet

all in her head

Old man says,

“String-player

word-rapper

drum-beater

Make the music.

Our house is your house

A place to be.”

The three smilin’

Ramone

Willie

Yock

Rockin'

Tumblin'

Slidin'

Shiftin'

Rollin'

Rhythm

Goin' at it

over

over

Better

Better

A group called

Squeezed

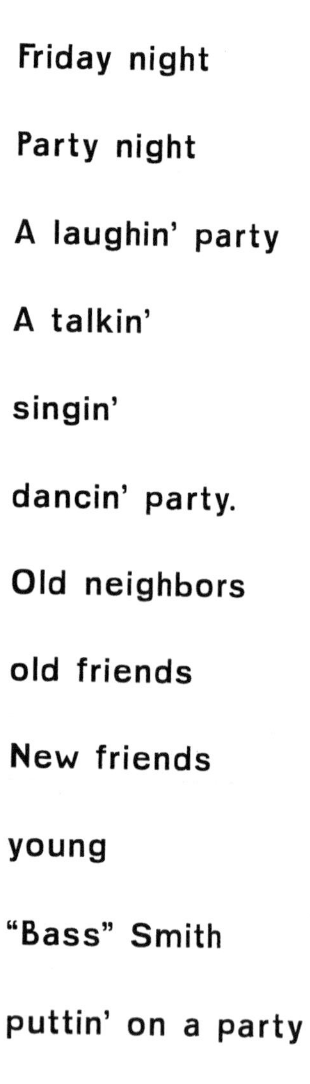

Friday night

Party night

A laughin' party

A talkin'

singin'

dancin' party.

Old neighbors

old friends

New friends

young

"Bass" Smith

puttin' on a party

Ramone

Willie

Yock

settin' up to play

sweatin' hands

cold on a warm night.

Fear

Willie's eyes wide

in a dark

scared face

Yock's finger tappin'

on jean-covered

thighs

Ramone's smile not real

crooked

tight

Arms up

"Bass" Smith shouts,

"These here my three

music-makers

storytellers

playin'

rappin'

rockin'

soundin' good, kids"

Ramone's fingers flyin'

slip

slidin'

pluckin'

good rhythm sound

Yock's sticks jumpin'

boom

bang

boomin'

Willie's rappin'

story 'bout a girl named

Tish.

Mr. Smith

spinnin' his bass

joinin' in

slither

pluck

boom

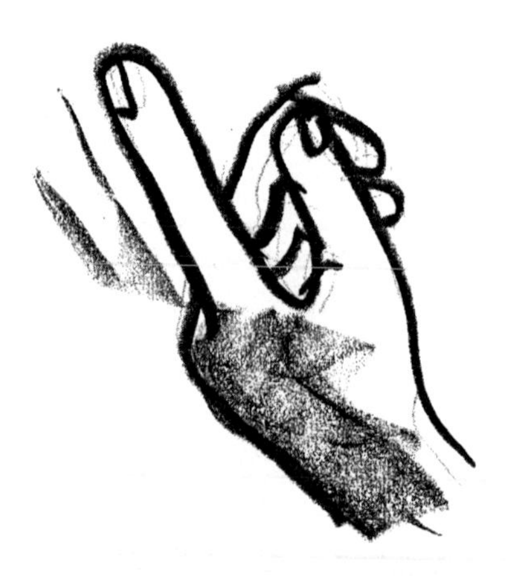

new sound

good sound

Ramone ticklin' the guitar

Willie talkin' the rap

Yock hammerin' the drums

Mr. Moses "Bass" Smith pluckin'

the bass

Three kids smilin'

Mr. Moses Smith smilin'

high fivin'

bein' proud.

A group called Squeezed.

LaVergne, TN USA
20 February 2011

217165LV00001B/4/P

9 781442 429444